Rabbit, Hare, and BUNNY

by Robert Broder ～ illustrated by Bryan Langdo

Ripple Grove
Press

First Edition 2019

ISBN 978-0-9990249-6-6
Library of Congress Control Number 2018963434
2 4 6 8 10 9 7 5 3 1
Printed in China

Creative Director: Robert Broder
This book was typeset in Baskerville.
The illustrations were rendered in watercolor and ink.

Ripple Grove
Press

Shelburne, Vermont
RippleGrovePress.com

Thank you for reading.

For the roommates I have liked
(and those I have not).—R. B.

For my family, my current "roommates."
We can all be a bit Bunny sometimes.—B. L.

RABBIT, HARE, AND BUNNY are roommates.

Rabbit is neat.

Hare is organized.

Bunny is disheveled.

Rabbit likes classical music.

Hare likes jazz.

Bunny likes anything with a banjo.

Being roommates, they have to share chores, like . . .

cleaning the bathroom,

paying the bills,

doing the dishes,

and taking out the trash.

As roommates, it's important to . . .
be considerate when someone has a friend over,

be respectful during someone's quiet time,

and be aware when others are waiting.

Rabbit and Hare tried to talk to Bunny about being mindful of others, but Bunny was still Bunny.

So they asked him to move out.

"I'm sorry but you haven't been listening," said Hare.
"And we're frustrated," said Rabbit.

"Oh. I see," said Bunny.

Bunny moved back in with his parents.

Rabbit and Hare interviewed for a new roommate.
First they met Possum.

"Do you like to play dead?" asked Possum.
"Um. No!" Rabbit and Hare answered at the same time.

Then they met Owl.

"So tell us about yourself," said Hare.
"Hoo," said Owl.
"You," said Rabbit. "What kind of hobbies do you have?"
"Hoo," said Owl.
"You! We're talking to you!" said Hare, getting frazzled.

Next came Fox.

"I can move in right away," said Fox.
"We'll get back to you," said Rabbit.
"Not!" said Hare as he slammed the door shut.

They were excited about Penguin.

"So, where are you from?" asked Hare.
"What kind of music do you like?" asked Rabbit.

But Penguin just sat there and said nothing.

And then came Bear.

"This place is awesome!" said Bear. "The couch is *soooo* comfy."

Rabbit and Hare were starting to realize that good roommates are hard to find.

Meanwhile, Bunny's parents were happy to have him back.

He ran errands with his mom.

"Bunny! Do you need new underwear?!"

His dad turned Bunny's room into a gym.

"Can you grab your old man a towel?"

Bunny went with his mom to yoga.

He waited while his dad got a haircut.

"I used to sing doo-wop on this street corner."

Even though Bunny loved his parents,
he was older now and missed living
with his friends.

A few weeks had gone by when Rabbit and Hare
bumped into Bunny at the coffee shop.

It was awkward at first, but after a few minutes, it wasn't.

"We miss you," said Rabbit and Hare.
"I miss you too," said Bunny.
"Would you like to move—"
"Yes!" responded Bunny.

Bunny was now more thoughtful of Rabbit and Hare.

And Rabbit and Hare let Bunny be himself.